Edward A. Claypool

The Scotch Ancestors of William McKinley

President of the United States

Edward A. Claypool

The Scotch Ancestors of William McKinley
President of the United States

ISBN/EAN: 9783337403218

Printed in Europe, USA, Canada, Australia, Japan

Cover: Foto ©Raphael Reischuk / pixelio.de

More available books at **www.hansebooks.com**

THE

SCOTCH ANCESTORS

OF

WILLIAM McKINLEY,

PRESIDENT OF THE UNITED STATES.

COMPILED BY

EDWARD A. CLAYPOOL,

A CHICAGO GENEALOGIST

CHICAGO, U. S. A.

1897.

Printed by SCHULKINS & CO., 196-198 Clark Street, Chicago.

This line of descent down to and including number 22 is fully substantiated by the Scottish chronicles and histories of the Highland Clans. There are differences in the manuscript genealogies left by the old Sean-a-chaidh, or historians of the Clans which may never be definitely adjusted, but I have used only such statements as I believe can be substantiated by historical data. From number 22 to number 27, I have relied principally upon printed, written, and oral statements of members of the present "Clan MacKinlay" of the United States and Canada, some of whom have spent years ferreting out the Clan genealogy. From number 27 to President McKinley, I am especially indebted to Mr. E. W. Spangler for data from the records of York County, Pennsylvania, and to Judge John S. Goodwin, Historian of the Clan MacKinlay, for later data. Mr. Wm. E. W. MacKinlay, Assistant Historian of the Clan, has lent invaluable aid throughout the whole line.

I would also acknowledge the courtesies extended by the efficient librarians of the Newberry Library and Chicago Public Library.

Few people realize that Chicago is rapidly becoming the recognized library center of this continent. *The New York Outlook* says: "Chicago libraries are greater in extent and endowment than those of any other American city."

This might, by some, be considered an extravagant statement, but it is fully substantiated by the recent report to the Chicago Board of Trade by its secretary, Mr.

George F. Stone, who has spent some time in collecting the statistics. The total number of bound volumes in our public libraries is 706,000, to which may be added 160.000 volumes in our semi-public institutions, making 866.000 bound volumes. These figures do not include the pamphlets, which would swell the number to over 2,000,000 titles, nor the valuable libraries of Evanston, Oak Park and other suburban towns. When it is considered that the growth of these libraries practically dates from the great fire of 1872, it is indeed a phenominal growth, and with another twenty-five years of like progress Chicago will compete favorably with the libraries of the Old World.

As a genealogy of the entire MacKinlay-McKinley McGinley family is contemplated, all descendants of the families will confer a favor on their posterity by sending copies of their family records.

Would also like records and addresses of all descendants of the Claypoole, Claypool or Claypole families.

EDWARD A. CLAYPOOL,
Genealogist.

284 East Huron Street
Chicago, U. S. A.

SYNOPSIS

of the

Line of Descent of President McKinley

from

MacDuff, Thane of Fife.

❀ ❀

1. DUNCAN MACDUFF, Maormor of Fife, born about A. D: 1000; killed Macbeth Dec. 5, 1056.

> " Lay on Macduff!
> And damn'd be him that first cries 'Hold enough!' "
> —Shakespeare's Macbeth.

2. DUFAGAN MACDUFF, styled 2nd Earl of Fife.

3. CONSTANTINE MACDUFF, styled 3rd Earl of Fife, died 1129. Justiciary of Scotland "a discreet and eloquent man."

4 GILLIMICHAEL MACDUFF, 4th Earl of Fife, died 1139.

5. DUNCAN MACDUFF, 5th Earl of Fife, Regent of Scotland, 1153, died 1154.

6. SEACH (Gaelic for SHAW) MacDuff, (died 1179). Commander of the army of King Malcolm IV, which quelled the Insurrection of Moray 1161. Called Mac-an-Toi-sic (son of the chief or foremost) which became the sirname of the family. Founder and first chief of Clan MacIntosh. Married Giles, daughter of Hugh de Montgomery and had

7. SHAW OIG (the younger) MacIntosh, (died 1209 or 1210). Second Chief of Clan MacIntosh and Governor of the Castle of Inverness for 30 years. Battle of Torvain. Married Mary, daughter of Sir Harry de Sandylands and had three sons of whom

8. WILLIAM MacIntosh married Beatrix Learmonth and had

9. SHAW MacIntosh, 4th Chief of MacIntosh. who married in 1230, Helena, daughter of William, Thane of Calder, and died in 1265. "Cumhadh mhic a' Arisaig."

10. FARQUHAR MacIntosh. (killed in duel 1274,) 5th Chief of Clan MacIntosh; MacIntosh war cry "Loch na Maoidh." Married Mora of Isla. daughter of Angus Mor and sister of Angus Oig the "Protector of Bruce."

11. ANGUS MacIntosh or Angus mac Farquhard, born 1268, died 1345, married in 1291-2, Eva daughter and heiress of Gillipatrick, the son of Dugall Dall who

was son of Gillichattan-Mor the founder of Clan Chattan and became Captain or leader of the Clan. Angus was a staunch supporter of Robert Bruce and took part in the famous battle of Bannockburn, in 1314.

12. IAN (Gaelic for JOHN) MacINTOSH.

13. GILCHRIST MacINTOSH, sometimes called Christi-Jonson or Gilchrist mac Ian (Gilchrist, son of John from which comes the name of Johnson.)

14. SHAW MOR (Great) MacINTOSH, or Mackintosh, whose pedigree is given in the ancient manuscripts as Shaw mac Gilchrisht mac Ian mac Angus mac Farquhar, etc., (Mac being the Gaelic for son,) was leader of the victorious thirty at the battle of the North Inch of Perth, 1396, which Sir Walter Scott so graphically describes in his "Fair Maid of Perth."

15. SEUMAS (JAMES) MACKINTOSH, the Chief of the Clan, killed at memorable battle of Harlaw, 1411, "the final contest between the Celt and Teuton for Scottish independence." Ballad: "There was not sin' King Kenneth's days, etc."

16. ALLISTER CIAR MACKINTOSH obtains the estate of Rothiemurchus by deed 1464 and is called "Shaw of Rothiemurchus;" married a daughter of "Stuart of Kinkardine."

13—

17. FEARCHARD (FARQUHAR) MACKINTOSH, forester to the Earl of Mar, appointed Hereditary Chamberlain of the Braes of Mar, 1460-1488. Married a daughter of Patrick Robertson first of the family of Lude, Chief of Clan Robertson or Clan Donnachie, descendant of "Erle Patryk de Atholia." His sons called Farquhar-son.

18. DONALD FARQUHARSON. The Piobrachd. Rallying cry of Clan Farquharson, "Carn na Cuimhne." Motto: "Fide et Fortitudine." Married a daughter of Robertson of the Calvene family.

19. FARQUHAR BEG (Gaelic for little,) married into the family of Chisholm, of Strath Glass, Erchless Castle, the family seat.

20. DONALD FARQUHARSON married Isabel, only child of Duncan Stewart, commonly called Duncan Downa Dona, of the family of Mar.

21. FINDLAY (Gaelic FIONN-LAIDH), commonly called FINDLA MOR, or Great Findla.
    Killed at the battle of Pinkie, 1547, while bearing the Royal Standard of Scotland. First wife a daughter of Baron Reid, of Kinkardine Stewart, by whom he had four sons, who took the name of MacIanla. The Gaelic form MacFhionn-laidh (meaning son of Findlay), being pronounced as nearly as English spelling can show it—Mac-ionn-lay, or Mach-un-la. Clan MacKinlay Suaich-ean-tas, or badge is Lus-nam-

ban-sith, the fox glove. Old motto of the clan: "*We force nae friend, We fear nae foe.*" Tartan or plaid.

22. WILLIAM MACKINLAY died in the reign of James VI. (1603-1625). Had four sons, who settled at "The Annie," a corruption of the Gaelic An-abhain-fheidh, meaning "The ford of the stag," which is near Callender, in Perthshire.

23. THOMAS (?) MACKINLAY, or at least one of the sons of William No. 22, the eldest of whom was John. Thomas is known to have lived at "The Annie" in 1587.

24. DONALD or DOMHNIUL MAC KINLAY, who was born at "The Annie," is known to have been a grandson of William No. 22.

25. JOHN (Gaelic IAN) MACKINLAY, born at "The Annie" about 1645; had three sons; Donald, the eldest, born 1669. "James, the Trooper" (born probably 1671), and John, born 1679.

26. "JAMES, THE TROOPER," went to Ireland as guide to the victorious army of William III. at the Battle of the Boyne, 1690. Settled in Ireland, and was ancestor of a large portion of the Irish McKinleys.

27. DAVID MCKINLEY, known as "David, the Weaver," born probably in 1705; exact date of his immigration to America not known, as the records of New Castle, Delaware, where most of the early Pennsylvania settlers landed, were destroyed by the British during the Revolutionary War. He settled in Chanceford Town-

ship, York County, Pa., probably before 1745, in which year a tract of land was granted to him. He died in 1761.

28. JOHN MCKINLAY died in 1779. Served in the Revolutionary War in 1778, in Capt. Joseph Reed's Company, York County Militia.

29. DAVID MCKINLAY, born May 16, 1755, in York County, Pa.; died Aug. 8, 1840, in Crawford County, Ohio. Served in the Revolutionary War in the companies of Captains McCaskey, Ross, Laird, Reed, Holderbaum, Sloymaker, Robe and Harnahan.
As a member of the "Flying Camp" he was engaged in the defense of the fort at Paulus Hook (now Jersey City, N. J.), and skirmish at Amboy in 1776, and in the skirmish at Chestnut Hill in 1777.
He married in Westmoreland County, Pa., Sarah Gray.

30. JAMES MCKINLEY, born Sept. 19, 1783. Married "Polly" Rose about 1805. Resided in Mercer County, Pa. Became interested in the iron business early in "the thirties." and run a charcoal furnace for a number of years at Lisbon, Ohio. Elder in the Lisbon Presbyterian Church from 1822 to 1836.

31. WILLIAM MCKINLEY, born in Pine Township, Mercer County, Pa., Nov. 15, 1807; died in 1892. Manager of the old furnace near New Wilmington, Lawrence County, Pa., for twenty-one years. Married Nancy

Allison in 1829. and resided at Poland, Ohio.   Was a
devout Methodist, a staunch Whig, a good Republican
and an ardent advocate of a protective tariff.

32.   WILLIAM McKINLEY, born Jan. 29, 1843, at Niles, O.
Attended Poland Academy.   Entered Allegheny College 1860.   Private 23d Ohio Volunteer Infantry June,
1861.   Shouldered the musket, carried the knapsack,
and "Drank from the same canteen."   Promoted to
Commissary Sergeant August, 1862; Second Lieutenant, September, 1862; First Lieutenant, February 7,
1863; Captain, July 25. 1864: Brevet Major of the
United States Volunteers, 1864.   Mustered out with
the 23d Ohio July 26, 1865.   Admitted to the bar,
1867; Prosecuting Attorney. 1869.   Married January
25, 1871, Miss Ida Saxton.

Defended coal miners of Stark County 1875. clearing
them of an unjust charge.

Elected to Congress 1876, and served fourteen years.
Governor of Ohio 1891 and 1893.   Elected President
of the United States 1896.

MAC DUFF.

(From an original sketch by R. R. McIan, Esq.)

Mr. James Logan, in "The Clans of the Scottish Highlands," says: "The figure is not only a Mac Duff, but he is Duff himself, as it is observable, those of this Clan, agreeably to their designation, usually are. (Duff being from the Gaelic Dubh, black or dark-colored man). He wears mogans or knit stockings, without feet, by no means an uncommon covering, which is used more for the purpose of protecting the legs from the prickly shrubs than as appurtenances of dress, and he appears furiously breasting up a hill in pursuit of some one with whom he has 'a reckoning to clear.'"

LINE OF DESCENT

OF

WILLIAM McKINLEY,

TWENTY-FIFTH PRESIDENT OF THE UNITED STATES,

FROM

MacDUFF, THANE OF FIFE.

*

"Before my body
I throw my warlike shield; Lay on Macduff!
And damn'd be him that first cries 'Hold enough!"
— Shakespeare's Macbeth

*

1. Duncan MacDuff.

Maormor (Gaelic maor, steward; mor, great, or great steward) of Fife, the celebrated Thane, of Shakespeare, was greatest and chief of those who labored to restore Malcolm Cean mor or King Malcolm III. to his throne, which had been usurped by Macbeth.

Holinshed, a Scottish chronicle of the 16th century, says:

" Makduffe, to anoid perill of life, purposed with himselfe to passe into England to procure Malcolme Cammore to claime the crown of Scotland." " Immediately then Makbeth most cruellie caused the wife and children of Makduffe, with all others whom he found in the castell, to be slaine."

—19

"But Makduffe was alreadie escaped out of danger, and gotten into England unto Malcolme Cammore, to trie what purchase hee might make by means of his support to reuenge the slaughter so cruellie executed on his wife, his children, and other friends."

"At his comming vnto Malcolme, he declared into what great miserie the estate of Scotland was brought, by the detestable cruelties exercised by the tyrant Macbeth, having committed many horrible slaughters and murders, both as well of the nobles as commons, for which he was hated right mortallie of all his liege people, desiring nothing more than to be deliuered of that intollerable and most heauie yoke of thraldom."

* * * * * Though Malcolme was verie sorowfull for the oppression of his countriemen the Scots, in manner as Makduffe had declared, yet doubting whether he was come as one that meant vnfein-edlie as he spake, or else as sent from Makbeth to betraie him, he thought to have some further triall."

Malcolm then gaue various long excuses and pictured himself as sensual, avaricious, deceitful, and unfit to govern the people.

"Then said Makduffe : * * Oh, ye unhappie and miserable Scotishmen, which are thus scourged with so manie and sundrie calamities, ech one above other ! Ye have one curssed and wicked tyrant that now reigneth over you without anie right or title, oppressing you with his most bloudie crueltie. This other that hath the right to the crowne, is so replet with the inconsistant behauiour and manifest vices of Englishmen, that he is nothing woorthie to enjoy it : for by his own confession he is not onelie avaritious, and given to vnsatiable lust, but so false a traitor withall, that no trust is to be had vnto anie woord he speaketh. Adieu, Scotland, for now I account myself a banished man for euer, without comfort or consolation : and with those woords the brackish teares trickled downe his cheekes verie abundantlie."

"At last, when he was readie to depart, Malcolme tooke him by the sleeue, and said : ' Be of good comfort, Makduffe, for I have none of these vices before remembered, but have jested with thee in this manner, onlie to prooue thy mind : for diuerse times heeretofore hath Makbeth sought by this manner of meanes to bring me into his hands. but the more slow I have shewed my selfe to con-descend to thy motion and request, the more diligence shall I vse in accomplishing the same.' "

* * * * * " Makbeth recoiled backe into Fife, there purposing to abide in campe fortified, at the castell of Dunsinane and to fight with his enemies, * * * he had such confidence in his prophesies, that he beleeued he should never be vanquished, till Birname wood were brought to Dunsinane."

* * * * * " Malcolme following hastilie after Mak-beth, came the night before the battell vnto Birname wood, and when his armie had rested a while there to refresh them, he commanded eurie man to get a bough of some tree or other of that wood in his hand, as big as he might beare, and to march foorth therewith in such wise, that on the next morrow they might come closelie and without sight in this manner within viewe of his enemies. On the morrow when Makbeth beheld them coming in this sort, he first marvelled what the matter ment, but in the end remembered himselfe that the prophesie which he had heard long before that time of the comming of Bir-name wood to Dunsinane castell, was liklie to be now fulfilled."

" Nevertheless, he brought his men in order of bat-tell, and exhorted them to doo valiantlie, howbeit his enimies had scarcely cast from them their boughs, when Makbeth perceiuing their numbvrs, betooke him streict to flight, whom Makduffe pursued with great hatred euen till he came vnto Lunfannaine, where Makbeth perceiuing that Makduffe was harde at his backe, leapt beside his horsse, saicing, ' Thou traitor, what meaneth it that thou shouldest thus in vaine follow me that am not appointed

to be slaine by anie creature that is borne of a woman,
come on, therefore, and receiue thy reward which thou
hast deserued for thy paines,' and therewithall he lifted
vp his swoord thinking to have slaine him."

"But Makduffe quicklie avoiding from his horsse, yer
he came at him, answered (with his naked swoord in his
hand) saieing, 'It is true, Makbeth, and now shall thine
insatiable crueltie haue an end, for I am even he that thy
wizzards haue told thee of. who was never borne of my
mother, but ripped out of her wombe :' therewithal he
stept vnto him and slue him in the place."

"Then cutting his head from his shoulders, he set it
vpon a pole and brought it vnto Malcolme. This was the
end of Makbeth, after he had reigned 17 years ouer the
Scotishmen."

[This chronicle is the foundation of Shakespeare's
tragedy of Macbeth.]

Macduff slew Macbeth at Lumplanan in Aberdeenshire,
Scotland, December 5th, 1056, and in reward for his
valuable services, King Malcolm III., bestowed on him
the following extraordinary privileges, as given in the
Buik of the Chroniclis of Scotland :

" To gude Makduffe the erle of Fyffe gaif he
Ane priuledge, and his posteritie ;
The first quhilk wes ane priuledge cond[ing,[1]
The erll of Fyffe quhen crownit wes the king,
Onto his chyre suld him convoy and leid,
The croun of gold syne[2] set vpoun his heid
With his awin hand, all seruice for to mak,
As president[3] most princinall of that act ;
The secund wes, that battell in ilk[4] steid
In his gyding the vangard for to leid ;
The thrid also, that neuir ane of his clan
Suld judgit be wnder ane vther man.
Quhair euir he war, bot with the erle of Fyffe.
Quhen that he war accusit of his lyffe.

---

1. Condign, worthy. 2. Since or afterwards. 3. Precedent. 4. Each

—22

Or in modern English: First, that he and his successors, lords of Fife, should have the right of placing the Kings of Scotland on the throne at their coronation. Second, that they should lead the van of the Scottish armies whenever the royal banner was displayed. Third, that if he or any of his kindred committed slaughter of a suddenty they should have a peculiar sanctuary, girth, or asuylum, and obtain remission on payment of an eric or atonement in money to the relations of those slain, which, in Scottish law was called kimbot. He was also rewarded by having his county of Fife confirmed to him, and was created Earl in 1061.

According to Boetius and Fordun, he was eighth in descent from Fyfe MacDuff, a chieftain of great power and wealth, who lived about the year A. D. 800, and who afforded to Kenneth MacAlpin (Kenneth II) who was the first king of all Scotland, strong aid in establishing his right to the throne, A. D. 843, which resulted in the union of the Picts and Scots. In reward for these services Macduff received from the Monarch a very large tract of land which he called Fife (now Fifeshire), and over which he was appointed hereditary Thane.

2. Dufagan,

The son of Duncan Macduff, styled 2d Earl of Fife, was witness to many charters of King Alexander I., and was an assenter to a charter of that King, confirming the rights of the Trinity Church of Scone. His son,

3. Constantine Macduff,

Styled 3d Earl of Fife, and who is supposed to have been the first who adopted the title, is witness to a charter of the Monastery of Dunfermline. He is also spoken of as a great judge of Scotland. In the Registry of the Priory of St. Andrews, page 17, will be found the records of a trial over which Earl Constantine, "a discreet and eloquent man," presided as Justiciary of Scotland. This meeting must have taken place early in the reign of King David, as the signature of Earl Constantine is soon replaced in the charters by that of Earl Gillimichael.

He is said to have died in 1129, about five years after the accession of David the First to the throne. His eldest son,

4. Gillimichael Macduff,

Fourth Earl of Fife, is witness to the foundation charter of the Abbey of Holyroodhouse in 1128, and to several other charters of King David. He died in 1139, leaving two sons, viz.: Duncan, 5th Earl, and Hugo, ancestor of the Earl of Wemyss.

5. Duncan Macduff,

Fifth Earl of Fife, who died Anno 1154, is witness to several charters of King David I., and of Malcolm IV., and was a liberal benefactor of the Church.

In 1138 he is conjectured to have been one of the five hostages delivered by David I. to Stephen, King of England, that the terms of the truce concluded after the "Battle of the Standard" would be preserved by the Scots.

According to Wintoun, he was appointed. Regent of Scotland in the minority of Malcolm IV. It was under his guardianship the young Malcolm, then in his eleventh year, was sent by his grandfather, King David I., on a tour of Scotland, and in every district was proclaimed and received as heir to the Crown. David I. died in 1153, and Earl Duncan performed the ceremony of placing the youthful Malcolm on the inaugural chair, or sacred stone of Scone, at his coronation in 1154 Duncan's second son,

6. **Seach** (Gaelic for **Shaw**) **Macduff,**

Having accompanied his father and the Prince in their tour of Scotland, became a great favorite of King Malcolm IV. In 1154 he is said to have had command of the army of Malcolm. For his assistance in quelling an insurrection among the inhabitants of Moray in 1161, the King made him Governor of Inverness, and presented him with the lands of Petty and Breachly, and the Forest of Strathearn.

From the high position of his father he was styled by the Gaelic speaking population Mac-an-Toi-sich (son of the chief or foremost), which became the surname of the family. Dr. John MacPherson observes that "as Malcolm Cean Mor gave a right to those powerful Thanes to lead the van, the name is, in a manner, accounted for." He was the founder and first Chief of Clan MacIntosh. He married Giles, daughter of Hugh de Montgomery, one of his comrades in the Moravian insurrection in 1161, and had three sons, Shaw, Malcolm and Duncan. He died in 1179, and was succeeded by his eldest son.

7. Shaw (Oig) MacIntosh,

Who was the second Chief of the Clan and Governor at the Castle of Inverness for thirty years, which he bravely defended when Thorfin, son of Harald MacMadach, the powerful Earl of Orkney and Caithness, made a raid into Inverness in 1196. His brother Duncan was slain during this raid at the battle of Torvain. He married Mary, daughter of Sir Harry de Sandylands, and had, I Fearchard (3d Chief of the Clan), II. William, and III. Edward, ancestor of Monivard

He died in 1209 or 1210, and was succeeded by his eldest son, Fearchard, who became third Chief of Clan MacIntosh, and took part in the expedition against Guthbred mac Donald mac William, in 1211, in Ross-shire. Fearchard died about 1240, without issue, and was succeeded as Chief of the Clan by his nephew, Shaw MacIntosh. (See No 9.)

8. William MacIntosh,

Second son of Shaw (or Shaw Oig, i. e , the younger). Married Beatrix Learmonth, a surname as old as the reign of Malcolm III., and from which descended Thomas Learmonth, better known as "Thomas the Rhymer," or "Thomas of Ercildoune," Scotland's earliest poet, who is supposed to have been born between 1226 and 1229 William is said to have resided at the Castle of Inverness with the other sons and grandsons of Shaw (Oig), and who defended it on numerous occasions against the marauding bands of the West. Some of them added considerable to the possessions of the family, which soon took firm root in the North.

9. Shaw MacIntosh,

Son of William, at the death of his uncle, Shaw (Oig), became fourth Chief of the MacIntoshes. The *war cry* of this Clan was "Loch na Maoidh" (Loch Moy, "the lake of threatening"), a small lake near the seat of the Chief in Inverness-shire.

The Cumhadh mhic a' Arisaig, or MacIntosh's Lament, is extremely plaintive and expressive. It is one of the most touching of that species of music, and a great favorite of the pipers.

Shaw married in 1230 Helena, daughter of William, Thane of Calder. He is mentioned as having acquired a lease of Rothiemurchus in Strath-spey, but the date is not given. The lands of Rothiemurchus, having been granted by King Alexander II. to Andrew, Bishop of Moray, Anno 1226, were held by the Bishops in lease by the Shaws during a hundred years without disturbance.

Prior to 1396 the Clan represented by the MacIntoshes had been (as was common amongst the Clans) often designated as the Clan Shaw, after the successive chiefs of that name, and sometimes, as the Clan of the Mac-an-Toisheach, i. e., the Thane's son.

Shaw died in 1265, and was succeeded by his son,

10. Farquhar MacIntosh,

Who as fifth Chief, fought at the head of his clan at the battle of Largs, October 3rd, 1263, where Haco IV, King of Norway was defeated. He was killed in a duel in 1274. He married Mora, daughter of Angus Mor of Isla, and sister of Angus Oig, who at the head of his clan (Clan Donald or MacDonald) formed the reserve and "did battle stalwart and stout on that never-to-be-forgotten day" at Bannockburn.

In 1306 Angus received Bruce into his castle of Dunaverty and protected him for nine months in his country of Rachlin, Isla and Uist. In consequence of this fidelty King "Robert the Bruce" bestowed upon him the post of honor, the right hand; and it was to this Angus that he addressed the words "My hope is constant in thee," on his making the final charge on the English.

11. Angus MacIntosh.

> "At Bannockburn I served the Bruce,
> Of whilk the Inglis had na russ."

Angus, often called Angus mac Fearchard (i. e , Angus, son of Farquhar), sixth Chief of Clan MacIntosh, was born in 1268, and died in 1345. In 1291-2 he married Eva, the daughter and heiress of Gillipatrick, the son of Dugall Dall, who was the son of Gillichattan-Mor, the founder of Clan Chattan (pronounced Kattan). By her he acquired the lands of Locharkeg, Glenluy and Strathlocie, which remained with the family until sold to Lochiel in 1665.

By this marriage he also acquired the station of Captain, or leader of Clan Chattan, which was the most powerful of the Highland Clans, being composed of the MacPherson, MacDuff, MacIntosh, MacBean, Shaw, Farquharson, MacGillivray, MacQueen, Clark, Davidson, Elder, and several others clans. Each clan had their own tartan and war cry, but all wore the Suaich-eantas or badge of Clan Chattan, viz., Lus na'n Craim-sheag na Bra-oi-laig, the red whortleberry (*vaccinium vitis idea*).

Angus was a chief of great activity, and a staunch supporter of King Robert, the Bruce with whom he took part in the famous battle of Bannockburn June 11, 1314, where the sturdy Scotts, with an army of not over 40,000 men (a number of historians say 30,000), completely routed Edward III. with a vast army of over 100,000, and thus virtually secured Scottish independence.

12. Ian (Gaelic for **John) MacIntosh,**

Or Mackintosh, as generally written by the modern historians. In charters granted by the lords of the Isles, and confirmed by King David II., the son of Eva, is designated as Captain of Clan Chattan, but whether *this* son or another, we know not.

13. Gilchrist MacIntosh,

Or Christi-Jonson, sometimes called Gilchrist mac Ian, i.e., Gilchrist, son of John, from whence comes the name Johnson.

14. Shaw Mor (Great) MacIntosh,

Or Mackintosh, whose pedigree is given in ancient manuscripts as Shaw, *mac* Gilchrist, *mac* Ian, *mac* Angus, *mac* Farquhar, etc. (*mac* being the Gaelic for "son"), was leader of the victorious Thirty at the North Inch of Perth, Sept. 5, 1396, before King Robert III., his Queen, and the Scottish nobility, which Sir Walter Scott so graphically describes in his "Fair Maid of Perth," and with less embellishment in his "Tales of a Grandfather.' The MacIntosh Mss. of 1500 states that Lauchlan, the old Chief of the MacIntoshes, gave Shaw a grant of Rothiemurchus "for his valour on the Inch that day." He died about 1405, and was buried in the churchyard of the parish, where his gravestone may still be seen. By a daughter of Duncan(?) "MacPherson of Clunie," he had seven sons, of whom the eldest,

15. Seumas (James) Mackintosh,

Chief of Clan Mackintosh, was killed at the memorable battle of Harlaw, which was fought on the eve of the feast of St. James the Apostle, July 24, 1411. "The Highlanders, who were ten thousand strong, rushed on with the fierce shouts and yells which it was their custom to raise in coming into battle, the English knights meeting them with ponderous maces and battle axes, which inflicted ghastly wounds upon their half armed opponents. The Constable of Dundee was slain, and the Highlanders, encouraged by his fall, wielded their broadswords and Lochaber axes with murderous effect, seizing and stabbing the horses and pulling down their riders, whom they dispatched with their daggers. The Highlanders left 900 men dead on the field of battle including the Chiefs Maclean and Mackintosh." The loss of the Highlanders was very small compared with that sustained by the Lowlanders. It was the final contest between the Celt and Teuton for Scottish independence, and from the ferocity with which it was waged and the dismal spectacle of war and bloodshed exhibited to the country, it made at the time an inconceivable impression on the national mind and is indelibly fixed in the music and poetry of Scotland.

A march called the " Battle of Harlaw," continued to be popular down to the time of William Drummond, of Hawthornden, the eminent Scottish poet (b. 1585, d. 1649).

A spirited ballad on the same event, describing the meeting of the armies and the deaths of the Chiefs, in no ignoble strain, is still recited by the bards.

' There was not, sin' King Kenneth's days,
    Sic strange intestine cruel strife
In Scotlande seen, as ilk man says,
    Where monie likelie lost their life:
Whilk made divorce 'tween man and wife.
And monie children fatherless,
    Whilk in this relm has been full rife:
Lord, help these lands! our wrongs redress!',

" In July, on Saint James his evin,
    That four-and-twenty dismal day.
Twelve hundred, ten score and eleven
    Of years sin' Christ, the soothe to say:
Men will remember, as they may.
    When thus the veritie they knaw:
And monie an ane will mourne for aye
    The brim battle of the Harlaw."

16. **Allister Ciar Mackintosh (Alexander,** Ciar, pronounced
    Kiar; the brown),

Son of Seumas, obtained the estate of Rothiemurchus
in Strath Spey, from Duncan, 11th Chief of Mackintosh,
by deed dated September 24th, 1464, and was often designated as Shaw of Rothiemurchus.

He married a daughter of "Stuart of Kinkardine"
and had four sons. the second being

17. **Fearchard (Farquhar) Mackintosh,**

Who was forester to the Earl of Mar, about 1440. and in
the reign of James III. (1460-1488), was appointed Hereditary Chamberlain of the Braes of Mar.

He married a daughter of Patrick, son of Robert, son
of Duncan d' Atholia a descendant of Patrick d' Atholia.
of whom Wyntoun says :

" A. D. 1391.   Erle Patrykl als is thidder gane.
                Wyth mony gud [men] of Lowthayne."

Patrick, Robert's son, was ancestor of the Robertsons of Lude, and the founder and Chieftain of the Clan Robertson, or Clan Donnachie, i. e., children of Duncan.

Fearchard's sons were called Farquhar-son, the first of the name in Scotland and the immediate ancestors of the Farquharsons of Invercauld, the main branch. His eldest son was,

18. Donald Farquharson.

> " How in the noon of night that pibroch thrills,
> Savage and shrill! But with the breath which fills
> Their mountain pipe, so fill the mountaineers
> With the fierce native daring which instils
> The stirring memory of a thousand years." *Byron.*

The piobrachd, as its name implies, is properly a pipe tune and is usually the Cruinneachadh, or gathering of a Clan, being a long piece of music composed on occasion of some victory or other fortunate circumstance in the history of a tribe which, when played, is a warning for the troops to turn out. There is, however, little attention now paid to the distinctions, and a piobrachd may be described as an extended piece of music adapted for the bagpipe, composed for the celebration of a battle where the Clan was successful, or before a conflict commenced, to excite the warriors to heroism. It was often played in the midst of a battle as an inspiration. These pieces become consecrated in the Clan to all succeeding enterprises of war and occasions of festive enjoyment.

The Cath-ghairm or rallying cry of Clan Farquharson was *Carn na Cuimhne*, the cairn of remembrance, an artificial heap of stones in Strathdee, around which the Clan assembled and on which the bard chanted the Brosnu cha' ca' or incentive to battle, before they departed.

The Farquharsons, according to Duncan Forbes, was "The only Clan family in Aberdeenshire." Their estimated strength was five hundred men, and they were among the most faithful adherents to the House of Stuart, and throughout all the struggles in its behalf, constantly acted up to their motto *Fide et fortitudine,* by faith and fortitude.

Donald married a daughter of Robertson of the Calvene family, and had an only son.

19. Farquhar Beg (Gaelic for little),

Who married into the Chisholm family of Strath Glass (Strath, valley, of the river Glass.) Erchless Castle the family seat, an old baronial mansion, situated in a picturesque locality in Strathglass or "Grey Valley," in Inverness-shire, is still occupied by the Chisholms.

Farquhar died there at the end of the reign of James III., leaving a numerous issue, of whom the eldest was,

20. Donald Farquharson,

Who married Isabel, the only child of Duncan Stewart, commonly called Duncan Downa Dona, of the family of Mar, and obtained by her the lands of Invercauld and Aberarder in 1520. He also gained considerable favors for faithful services rendered to the Crown. His son and successor,

21. Findlay (Gaelic Fionn=laidh),

Commonly called Fixdla Mor, or Great Findla, from his great size and strength, was killed at the battle of Pinkie Sept. 10, 1547, while bearing the Royal Standard of Scotland, and was buried in the Inveresk churchyard, near Edinburg. By his first wife, a daughter of Baron Reid, of Kinkardine Stewart, he had four sons, who took the name of Mac Ianla, the name being derived from Finlay, the Gaelic form of which is Fionn-ladh. The form Mac Fhionn-laidh (meaning son of Findlay), being pronounced as nearly as English spelling can show it— Mac-ionn-lay, or Mach-un-la.   **1159742**

The second wife of Findla Mor was Beatrix Gardyn, of Balchorie, by whom he had seven sons who retained the name of Farquharson. From the sons by his first wife sprang the Clan Fhinla, or MacKinlay, which was so closely allied to Clan Farquharson that they adopted the same war cry and badge.

The MacKinlay Suaicheantas, or badge, is Lus-nam-ban-sith, the foxglove.

The old motto of the clan was "*We force nae friend, we fear nae foe.*"

The MacKinlay tartan, or plaid, is the same as that of the Farquharsons, except the yellow lines are replaced by red lines.

22. William MacKinlay,

The eldest son of Findla Mor, died in the reign of James VI. (1603 1625). He had four sons, who settled at "The Annie," a corruption of the Gaelic An-Abhain-fheidh, meaning "The ford of the Stag," which is near Callender, in Perthshire. The estate is still occupied by their descendants.

23. Thomas (?) MacKinlay,

Or at least one of the above mentioned sons of William No. 22, the eldest of whom was John.

Thomas is known to have lived at "The Annie," in 1587, and

24. Donald, or Domhniul MacKinlay,

Who was born at "The Annie," is known to have been a grandson of William No. 22. His son.

25. John (Gaelic Ian) MacKinlay,

Who was born at "The Annie" about 1645, had three sons, viz.: Donald, the eldest, born 1669; "James, the Trooper," (born probably 1671), and John, born 1679.

26. "James, the Trooper,"

Went to Ireland acting as guide to the victorious army of William III. at the battle of the Boyne, July 1, 1690.

He married probably 1697 1700, and settled in Ireland, becoming the ancestor of a large portion of the Irish McKinleys.

At first it was supposed that James McKinley, born in Ireland in 1708, who settled in Pennsylvania, and died at the home of his great granddaughter, Mrs. Eleanor (Wiles) Goodwin, in Warren County, Ohio, in 1812, at the age of 104 years, was the ancestor of President McKinley, but later developments point to an elder son,

27. David McKinley,

Known as "David the Weaver," born probably 1705. The exact date of his immigration to America, and where he first settled, is not known. The early immigrants to Pennsylvania landed mostly at New Castle, Delaware, the early records of which were destroyed by the British during the Revolutionary War.

The records of York County, Pa., show that a warrant was issued to him in 1745 for a tract of land in Chanceford Township, York County, Pa., and he was there probably as early as 1743. He died before 1761, leaving one daughter and three sons, of whom

28. John McKinley,

Died in 1779. He served in the Revolutionary War in 1778, in the Company of Capt. Joseph Reed, ferryman, York County Militia. [Spangler's Annals, pp. 430-1.]

Of the five children who survived him, his son,

29. David McKinley

Was born May 16, 1755, in York County, Pa., and resided at Chanceford at the time of the Revolutionary War. He served seven months in Capt. W. McCaskey's Company, Col. Richard McAllister's Regiment of York County (Pa.) Militia, and was engaged in the skirmish at Amboy, July, 1776.

"I have sent orders to the commanding officer of the Pennsylvania Militia to march to Amboy.

July 14. 1776.   GEO. WASHINGTON."

Two companies of this militia which helped form the "Flying Camp" arrived at Amboy July 16, 1776, as reported by the commanding officer. [Am. Archives I., 330 and 369.]

David McKinley was also engaged with his company at the defense of the Fort at Paulus Hook (now Jersey City, N. J.).

Gen. Mercer, in his report to Congress Sept. 4, 1776, says:

"In obedience to orders from General Washington, between three and four thousand of the militia of Pennsylvania and New Jersey assembled at Bergen, ready to pass on to New York, but were countermanded on the retreat of the army from Long Island."

"We have, however, strengthened the posts at Powles Hook and Bergen Neck to the complement of twenty-five thousand men."

On the 15th of September the British captured New York City. In speaking of the bombardment of the city by the ships Roebuck, Phœnix and Tartar, *The Freeman's Journal* of Oct. 5, 1776, says the vessels "were roughly treated by the American battery at Paulus Hook."

Paulus Hook Fort was evacuated Sept. 23, 1776.

David also served in the companies of Captains Ross, Laird, Reed, Holderbaum, Sloymaker, Robe and Harnahan, and was engaged in the skirmish of Chestnut Hill in 1777.

As the statement that he served under eight different captains has been doubted, the following letter will add weight to the above statements:

DEPARTMENT OF THE INTERIOR,
BOARD OF PENSIONS.

DEAR SIR: WASHINGTON, D. C., April 6, 1895.
In reply to your request for a statement of the military history of David McKinley, a soldier of the Revolutionary War, you will find below the desired information as contained in his (or his widow's) application for pension on file in this bureau.

Date of Enlistment or Service Appointment	Length of Service	Rank	Captain	Colonel	State
June, 1776	7 months	Private	W. McCaskey	McCollister*	Pa
1777	2 "	"	Ross	Smith	"
1777	2 "	"	Laird	Not stated	
1777	2 "	"	Reed	Gen. Potter	
1778	2 "	"	Holderbaum	Elder	
1778	2 "	"	Sloymaker	Boyd	"
1778	2 "	"	Robe	Bar	"
1778	2 "	"	Harnahan	Not stated	"

Battles engaged in : Defense of fort at Paulus Hook, and skirmishes at Amboy and Chestnut Hill.
Residence at enlistment, Chanceford, Pa.
Date applied for pension, August 15, 1832.
Residence at date of application, New Lisbon, O.
Age of applicant, born May 16, 1755, in York Co., Pa.
Remarks : After the war, lived in Westmoreland, Co., Pa., fifteen years; then removed to Mercer County, and in 1814 settled in Columbiana Co., Ohio.

Very respectfully, WILLIAM LOCHREN,
Commissioner of Pensions.

*Should be McAllister. See Colonial Records of Pennsylvania. Vol. X., p. 682. viz:
"In Council of Safety. Aug. 13. 1776.
By order of the Board. John M. Nessbitt. Esq., Treasurer was directed to pay Captain Thomas Fisher £46.0.0. for Arms purchased and to be charged to Colonel Rich'd McAllister of York Co."

David McKinley died August 8, 1840, in Crawford County. O.

On December 9. 1780. he was married in Westmoreland County, Pa., to Sarah Gray. by whom he had ten children, the second being

30. James McKinley,

Born Sept. 19, 1783, who married "Polly" Rose about 1805. and resided on a farm in Pine Township, Mercer County, Pa. Early in "the thirties" he became interested in the iron business, and run a charcoal furnace for a number of years at Lisbon. O. He was an elder in the Lisbon Presbyterian Church from 1822 to 1836. during the pastorate of Rev. Dr. Vallandigham. His eldest son,

31. William McKinley,

Was born in Pine Township. Mercer County, Pa., Nov. 15. 1807. Having been trained in the iron business by his father, he, at an early age, became manager of the old furnace near New Wilmington. Lawrence County, Pa., which position he filled for twenty.one years. During that extended period he drove every Saturday to Poland, O., where his family had their home. returning on Monday to his duties at the furnace. He was a devout Methodist, a staunch Whig, a good Republican and an ardent advocate of a protective tariff He died in 1892 at the age of eighty-five.

He was married in 1829 to Nancy Allison, an estimable lady of Scotch-Irish blood, who bore him nine children, of whom the seventh child is

32. President William McKinley,

Who was born January 29, 1843, at Niles, Trumbull County, O., where his father was interested in one of the early iron furnaces of that section. He was educated in the common schools and at Poland Academy; at the age of seventeen he entered Allegheny College at Meadville, Pa., but taking sick early in the term he returned home, and that winter taught a country school near Poland, O. The following summer a new school was open for him Fort Sumpter's booming guns roused the blood of his liberty-loving Scotch ancestors (although he knew not of them), and in June, 1861, in response to Abraham Lincoln's first call for troops, he enlisted as a private soldier in the 23d Ohio Volunteer Infantry, and marched to the front. For fourteen months the young soldier served in the ranks. He shouldered his musket, carried the knapsack and "Drank from the same canteen." Every duty of the private soldier he faithfully performed. In camp, on march, on picket he bore his part, and the battles of Antietem and South Mountain only served to further rouse the blood of the descendant of the Highland Chiefs. He saw his first battle when Rosecrans defeated Floyd at Carnifex Ferry. His first promotion was that of Commissary Sergeant.

On Sept. 24, 1862, after the battle of Antietem, he was promoted to Second Lieutenant. "Blood will tell." In less than five months he takes another step up the ladder, and is promoted to First Lieutenant. On July 25, 1864, he is made Captain, speedily followed by promotion to the brigade and division staff of Gen. Rutherford B. Hayes; next as Acting Assistant Adjutant-General on the staff of Gen. George Crook, then on the staff of Major-Gen. Winfield S. Hancock, and subsequently on the staff of Gen. Samuel S. Carroll.

He was with Sheridan in his great campaign through the Shenandoah Valley.

Did he fight? A treasured document signed by Abraham Lincoln, which made William McKinley Brevet Major of the United States Volunteers in 1864 "for gallant and meritorious services at the battles of Opequan, Cedar Creek and Fisher's Hill," is an emphatic answer. In his "Memoirs," Gen. Sheridan tells how he found the young major rallying the troops at Cedar Creek on the morning of his famous ride from Winchester.

He was with the famous 23d Ohio in all its battles, and was mustered out with it July 26, 1865, after more than four years of hard, active and distinguished service.

After the war, he turned his attention to the study of law, and attended the Law School at Albany, N. Y. In 1867 he was admitted to the bar, and in 1869 was elected Prosecuting Attorney of Stark County, O., and served two years. About this time he attended another court, and did some courting which resulted in his marriage Jan. 25. 1871. to Miss Ida Saxton, a gentle and accomplished lady, the daughter of James A. Saxton, a prominent business man of Canton, O. This has been a very happy union, the devotion of husband and wife, constant, and a true representation of "The love that never grows old."

Two children were born to them, both of whom died young.

The kind heartedness of Major MacKinley was forcibly shown during the mining troubles of 1875. After a strike and riot in the western part of Stark County, the building over the coal shaft and other buildings had been burned, and thirty or forty of the strikers were indicted for the offense; Major McKinley believing they were unjustly treated and not guilty of destroying the works, took charge of the case, which is still looked back upon as one of the memorable criminal trials of Stark County, O.

The result was the acquittal of all but one of the accused, who was sentenced to three years in the penitentiary, but was pardoned by Governor Hays after hearing McKinley's appeal on his behalf.

When the miners called upon him with notes and drafts with which to pay him for his services, the Major told them that as they had been out of work and put to much expense by this charge, their families needed all they could earn, and he could better do without the money than they could ; that he had taken their case because he believed they had been grievously wronged, and he defended them more to secure justice than to make money.

He tore up the notes and drafts, and sent the men home to earn a living for their families. The miners of Eastern Ohio and Western Pennsylvania have never forgotten this kindness.

Major McKinley was elected to Congress in 1876 and served continuously in the House of Representatives until March, 1891, fourteen years. He served on the most important committees, and won distinction by his prominent and profound ability in the consideration and preparation of economic measures. He was elected Governor of Ohio in 1891, and as evidence of his just and able administration, he was re-elected in 1893 by the greatest number of votes ever cast for any State or Presidential candidate in the history of Ohio.

The bronze badge of the G. A. R., or the red, white and blue rosette of the Loyal Legion, is always seen in his button-hole.

President and Mrs. McKinley are members of the Methodist Episcopal Church.

During the campaign of 1894, one of the Nebraska Glee Clubs sang,

> " The man will fare slimly
> Who opposes McKinley
> In eighteen ninety six."

This proved a good prophecy, for on November 3, 1896, William McKinley was elected the twenty-fifth President of the United States by an overwhelming majority.

TARTAN OR PLAID.

The Tartan being, as it were, a Highlander's coat armour, he is especially careful that it shall in nowise be dishonored.

Mr. James Logan, an eminent authority on Scottish costumes, gives the following:

"A web of Tartan is two feet two inches wide, at least within half an inch, more or less. Commencing at the edge of the cloth, the depth of colours is stated throughout the square, on which the scale must be reversed or gone through again to the commencement."

Total width of pattern, 10 5-16 inches. ½ of an inch colors.

MacDuff Tartan.— 4 red, 3 azure, 4 black, 6½ green, 3½ red, 1 black, 3½ red, 1 black, 3½ red, 6½ green, 4 black, 3 azure, 8 red.

MacIntosh Tartan.—12 red, 6 blue, 2½ red, 10½ green, 4 red, 1½ blue, 4 red, 10½ green, 2½ red, 6 blue, 24 red.

The chief also wears a particular Tartan of a very showy pattern.

Farquharson Tartan.—1½ red, 2 blue, 1½ black, 1½ blue, 1½ black, 1½ blue, 4 black, 4 green, 1 yellow, 4 green, 4 black, 4 blue, 1½ black, 1 red.

MacKinlay Tartan.— Same as the Farquharson, except the yellow lines are replaced with red.